Hello, Family Members,

Learning to read is one of the [...] of early childhood. **Hello Rea** [...] children become skilled readers who like to read. Beginning readers learn to read by remembering frequently used words like "the," "is," and "and;" by using phonics skills to decode new words; and by interpreting picture and text clues. These books provide both the stories children enjoy and the structure they need to read fluently and independently. Here are suggestions for helping your child *before*, *during*, and *after* reading:

Before

- Look at the cover and pictures and have your child predict what the story is about.
- Read the story to your child.
- Encourage your child to chime in with familiar words and phrases.
- Echo read with your child by reading a line first and having your child read it after you do.

During

- Have your child think about a word he or she does not recognize right away. Provide hints such as "Let's see if we know the sounds" and "Have we read other words like this one?"
- Encourage your child to use phonics skills to sound out new words.
- Provide the word for your child when more assistance is needed so that he or she does not struggle and the experience of reading with you is a positive one.
- Encourage your child to have fun by reading with a lot of expression . . . like an actor!

After

- Have your child keep lists of interesting and favorite words.
- Encourage your child to read the books over and over again. Have him or her read to brothers, sisters, grandparents, and even teddy bears. Repeated readings develop confidence in young readers.
- Talk about the stories. Ask and answer questions. Share ideas about the funniest and most interesting characters and events in the stories.

I do hope that you and your child enjoy this book.

—Francie Alexander
  Chief Education Officer,
  Scholastic's Learning Ventures

For Lou Bonamarte—
anyone with a brush in each hand
can't be all bad!
—S.S. & J.B.

ISBN: 0-439-32315-0

Copyright © 2001 by Susan Schade and Jon Buller.
All rights reserved. Published by Scholastic Inc.
SCHOLASTIC, HELLO READER, CARTWHEEL BOOKS, and associated logos are trademarks and/or registered trademarks of Scholastic Inc.

Library of Congress Cataloging-in-Publication Data

Schade, Susan.
  Space Dog Jack and the haunted spaceship / by Susan Schade and Jon Buller.
    p. cm. — (Hello reader! Level 1)
  "Cartwheel books."
  Summary: On Halloween, Space Dog Jack comes to the aid of his friend Earth Dog Bob, who is being menaced by a Blob from outer space.
    ISBN 0-439-32315-0 (pbk.)
    [1. Dogs—Fiction. 2. Halloween—Fiction. 3. Science fiction. 4. Stories in rhyme.] I. Buller, Jon, 1943- II. Title. III. Series.
  PZ8.3.S287   Sp 2001
  [E]—dc21   2001020593

12 11 10 9 8 7 6 5 4 3   03 04 05

Printed in the U.S.A. 23
First printing, October 2001

SPACE DOG JACK
and the HAUNTED SPACESHIP

by Susan Schade and Jon Buller

Hello Reader! — Level 1

SCHOLASTIC INC.
New York   Toronto   London   Auckland   Sydney
Mexico City   New Delhi   Hong Kong

I'm Space Dog Jack
of Planet Woo.
A space-mail message
just came through.

HAVE NO FEAR,
I space-mail back.
I AM COMING.
YOUR FRIEND, JACK.

I land on Earth.
"Where's Bob?" I ask.

"It's me!" Bob says.
"In my Halloween mask!"

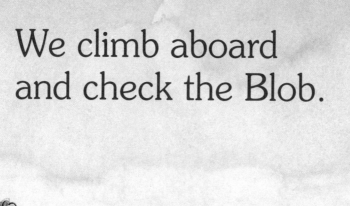

We climb aboard
and check the Blob.

I pull the black
Blob-Finder knob.

It bleeps and prints out:
NO BLOB FOUND.

"That's strange," I say.
"Let's look around."

We see a ship.
I get it now!
They're tricking us,
and I know how!

"It is not real,"
I say to Bob.
"It's just a <u>picture</u>
of a Blob!"

What is their plan?
We must find out.
We dock. We board.

"Game's up!" I shout.

It's silent.
There is no one there.

Just dust and cobwebs
everywhere.

Soft and low, we hear,
"Wooo-hoooo."

Then silence.
Then a sudden . . .

We scream! We jump!

"Ha-ha! Hoo-hoo!
We scared the Earth,
and we scared you!"

We run away,
but we are mad.

Scaring the whole Earth was bad!

They should not mess
with Bob and Jack.

We use Bob's mask.
We scare them back.

We chased those big space ghosts away. We're heroes back on Earth today!

Bob says to me,
"Why don't you stay
for Halloween?"
I say, "Okay!"

Bob wears his mask.
I wear a sheet.
And Bob and I go
trick-or-treat!